This **LITTLE TIGER** book

belongs to:

_____

_____

_____

For Alex H,
Amy and Millie
– F R

LITTLE TIGER PRESS
1 The Coda Centre, 189 Munster Road,
London SW6 6AW
www.littletiger.co.uk

First published in Great Britain 2016
This edition published 2017
Text and illustrations copyright © Fiona Ross 2016
Fiona Ross has asserted her right to be identified as the author and illustrator
of this work under the Copyright, Designs and Patents Act, 1988

A CIP catalogue record for this book is available from the British Library

Printed in China · LTP/1800/1434/0516

1 2 3 4 5 6 7 8 9 10

LITTLE TIGER PRESS
London

Hyde and Squeak

FIONA ROSS

Late at night,
if you hear a knock at
the door, it's best not to answer.
YOU wouldn't, would you? Because you
may just find a mysterious . . .

. . . BOX!

101

Congratulations!
1st Prize!

"Fancy that!"
gasped Granny.

"You've won another
competition!"

"Wowzers!"
thought Squeak.

PRIZE...
A HAMPER OF
PIES!!!

COMPETITION
TIME
WIN A LIFETIME
SUPPLY OF
LOO ROLL!

WIN A ONE WAY
TICKET INTO...
SPACE!!!

Squeak had won a wobbly jelly – but with a whiff of something beastly.

"Disgusting!" said Granny, and slung it in the bin.

But Squeak couldn't stop thinking about his icky, sticky prize.

Squeak grunted and growled.

He burped and slurped . . .

That night, when Granny was softly snoring, Squeak tiptoed downstairs. "I'll just have a taste," he thought. What a bad idea!

YUCK!

. . . Squeak turned into Hyde – a massive, messy

monster mouse!

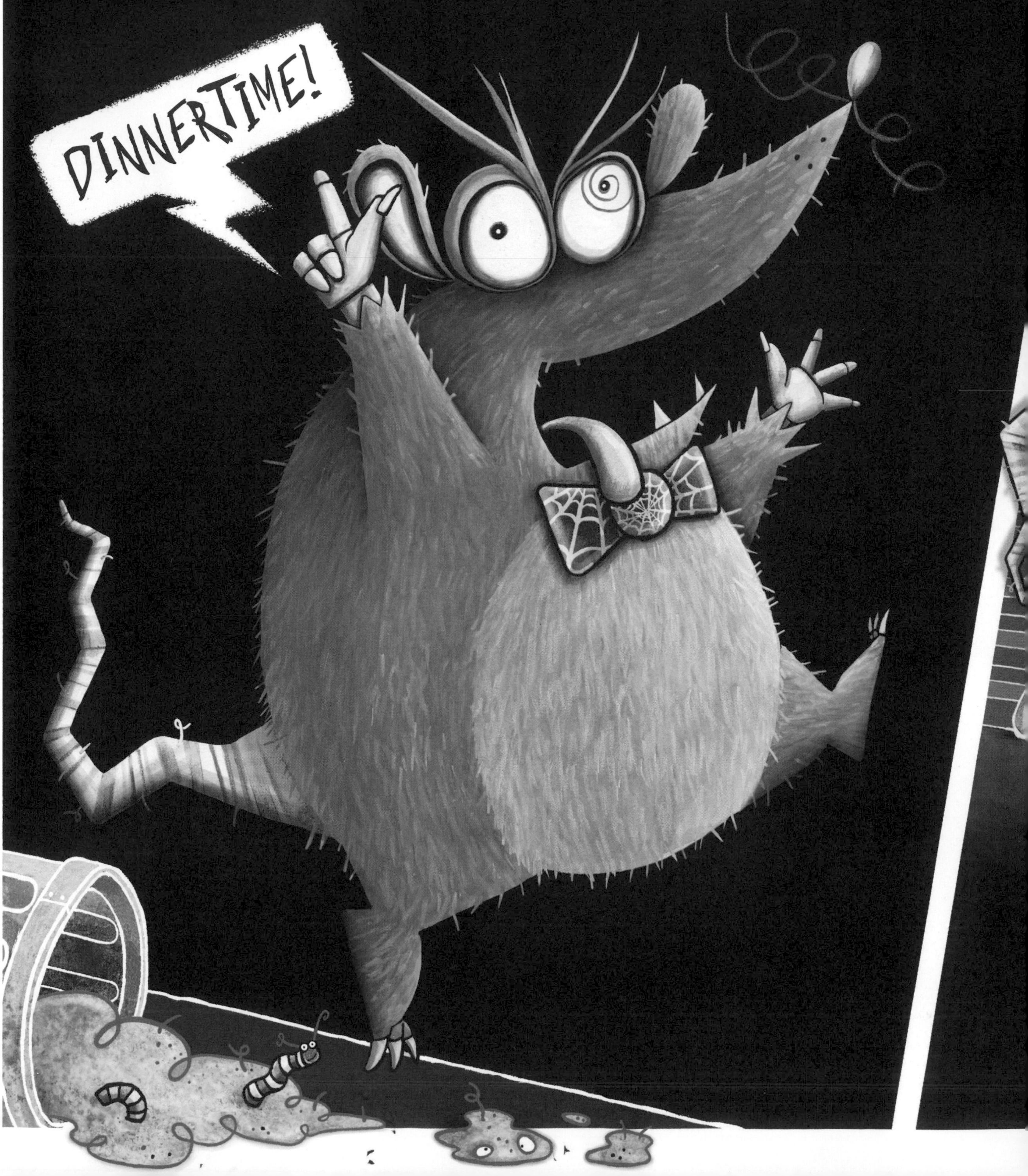

First he gobbled the food in the cupboards.

Then he guzzled the snacks in the fridge.

Every last one!

"I NEED MORE GRUB!" roared Hyde, and he telephoned for a super-sized supper.

But Hyde was on a mission.
ZAP IT & BAG IT
BANG!
CRASH!
ZAP IT & BAG IT
FIZZ!
FLASH!
In no time at all . . .

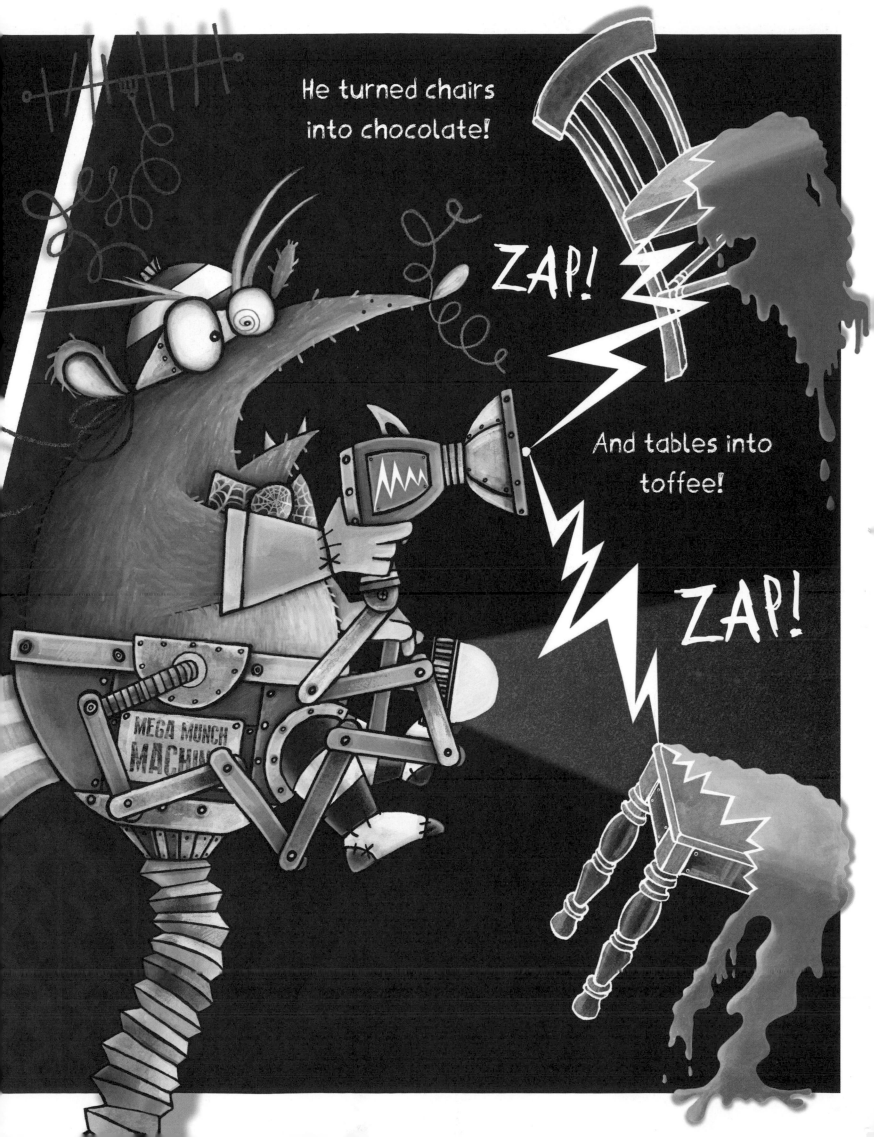

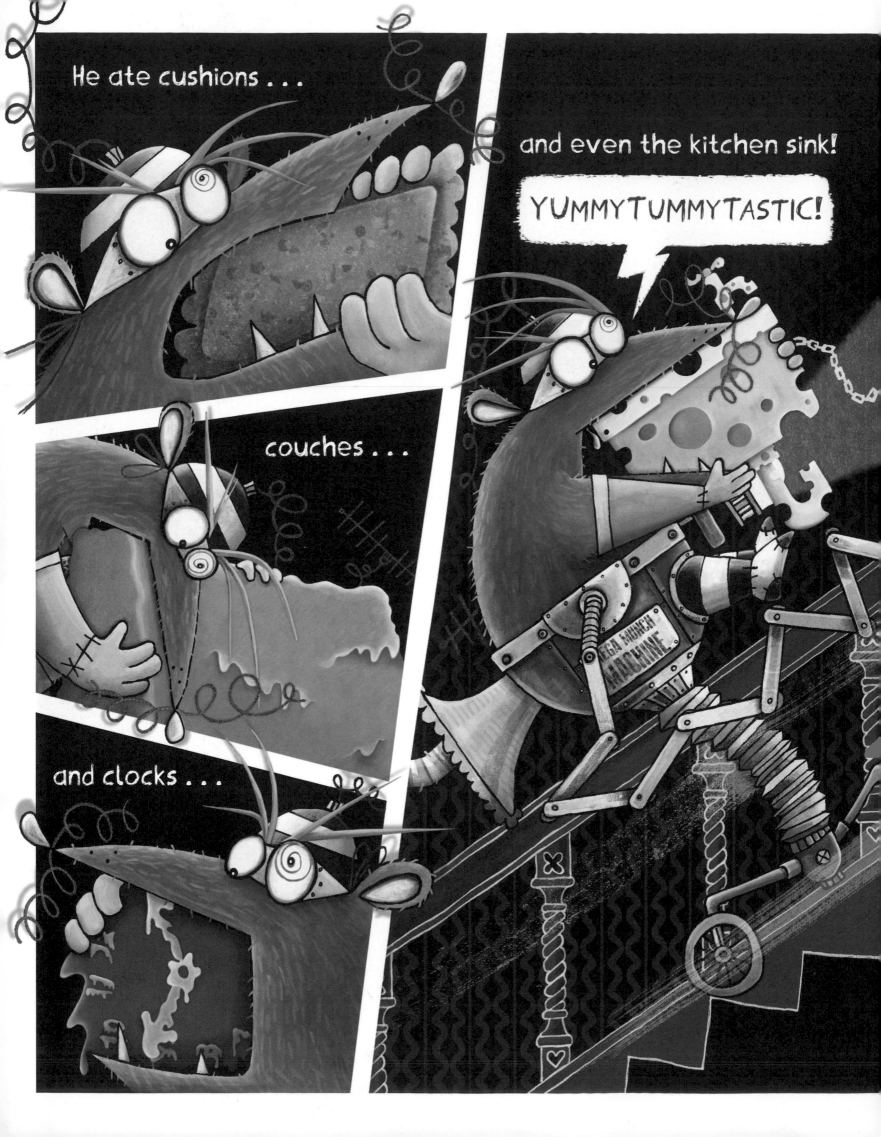

When Granny returned, everything was gone!
"Crumbs! What's happened here!" she gulped.
"And what's this strange machine?"

We know it was a monster's work . . .
But poor Squeak couldn't
remember a thing.

Not Granny!

"You want food? I'll GIVE you food!" she yelled. And she hurled a huge pineapple right into the zapper!

Then

PARP!

went Hyde.

POOF!

he disappeared.

PING!
Squeak was
back.

Soon things were almost back to normal.

Phew!

"My dear, dear Squeak!" cried Granny, and she jumped for joy to see him.

"I knew that jelly was trouble!" said Granny. "Let's not win any more of those!"

Squeak nodded.

No more jellies.

But he STILL loved a competition . . .

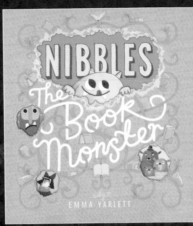

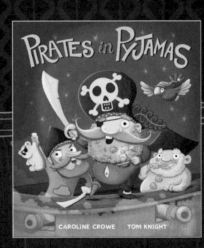